DANNY ORLIS
AND THE
MAN FROM THE PAST

DANNY ORLIS

AND THE
MAN FROM THE PAST

BERNARD PALMER

Danny Orlis and the Man from the Past
© 2023 by Bernard Palmer
All rights reserved. First edition 1959.
Second edition 2023.

Scripture quotations from The Authorized (King James) Version. Rights in the Authorized Version in the United Kingdom are vested in the Crown. Reproduced by permission of the Crown's patentee, Cambridge University Press.

Cover image: Adobe Firefly
Character illustrations: John Ball
Editor: Jon D. Fogdall

Aneko Press Youth

www.anekopress.com

Aneko Press, Life Sentence Publishing, and our logos are trademarks of Life Sentence Publishing, Inc.
203 E. Birch Street
P.O. Box 652
Abbotsford, WI 54405

JUVENILE FICTION / Religious / Christian / Action & Adventure
Paperback ISBN: 978-1-62245-980-3
eBook ISBN: 978-1-62245-981-0
10 9 8 7 6 5 4 3 2 1
Available where books are sold

CONTENTS

Ch. 1: An Unexpected Visitor.................................... 1

Ch. 2: The Visitor's Reason 11

Ch. 3: Angle Inlet 19

Ch. 4: A Charge to Danny.................................... 25

Ch. 5: A Thrilling Rescue 33

Ch. 6: The Letter from Mexico 43

Ch. 7: Harold Bauer Returns 49

Ch. 8: A Question for Ron 57

Ch. 9: Uncle Harold's Plans.................................... 65

Ch. 10: Flight to Winnipeg 75

Ch. 11: Discovered.................................... 83

Ch. 12: Ron's Discovery and Decision.................................... 93

CHAPTER 1

AN UNEXPECTED VISITOR

The warm spring sun had thawed the snow, leaving dirty little puddles scattered carelessly about the still-brown lawns. Mud was churned into hub-deep ruts in Cedarton's unpaved streets, and the streams were running bank full.

For all the evidence of spring, the thermometer plummeted at night. Danny Orlis buttoned his coat about his neck and picked his way over the freezing mud and up the street to the Meyers' home.

It was fairly late, and he thought the house would be dark, but to his surprise, there was a light in the living room and Mr. and Mrs. Meyer were waiting up for him.

He took off his coat and hung it in the hall closet.

"I didn't mean to be so late," Danny explained. "But Kay and I were cramming for exams."

Mr. Meyer put aside his paper.

"I just wanted to talk with you for a minute."

Danny crossed the room and sat down.

"Is something wrong?" he asked.

Mr. Meyer shook his head. "I don't suppose there is," he said. "But something happened today that has been bothering me."

Danny leaned forward. "Does it have to do with me?"

"Just before closing time this evening a guy came in pretending he wanted to buy something," the businessman went on. "But actually, he seemed more interested in prying. He asked a lot of personal questions about you and the twins."

Danny flinched. It was as though icy fingers grasped his stomach and squeezed it into a tight, hard knot.

"He seemed to know a good deal about all of you," Mr. Meyer continued. "He said it wasn't important, but he acted as though it was."

"Don't get Danny all excited," Mrs. Meyer said to her husband. "It was probably a friend from up where the twins and Danny live. I don't think it's anything to be alarmed about."

"Neither do I," her husband answered. "Still, he didn't ask the kind of questions a friend would ask. He wanted to know how long the twins had been down here with us. He wanted to know if they were properly cared for and what sort of grades they were getting in school. A friend doesn't ask that sort of questions."

Danny was silent.

"And besides, I didn't like the man's looks," the hardware dealer went on. "He didn't appear to me to be the type who would be particularly interested in a couple of kids."

Danny Orlis went to bed then, but he couldn't sleep. Questions went reeling through his mind. It had been several years since his parents adopted the twins, and they hadn't heard from any of the Bauer family since. Who could possibly be interested in Ron and Roxie?

The instant Danny Orlis awakened, he thought again of the stranger. At first, he planned to talk with Ron and Roxie, to warn them against him, but Mr. Meyer advised against it.

"There's no use in scaring them, Danny."

* * *

The month passed quickly, and almost before Danny realized it the finals were over and commencement exercises were to be held the following night.

Mr. and Mrs. Orlis came in by bus.

"Tex planned on flying us down," Mr. Orlis said, "but he got a hurried call to fly a couple of prospectors up north of Flin Flon and was afraid he wouldn't make it back."

"Am I ever glad to see you, Dad!" Danny said, telling him about the stranger. "I didn't know what to do."

Mr. Orlis didn't seem alarmed. "I don't see that we have anything to get excited about. The adoption papers are in order, so there isn't a thing, legally, that anyone can do."

Danny sighed his relief.

* * *

After commencement, Marilyn, Tim, Danny, and Kay got together outside the auditorium where the exercises had been held.

"Well, that's over," Danny said, grinning widely. "I finally made it."

"I don't feel like going home yet," Kay told him.

"Why don't we go over to Marilyn's basement and play Ping-Pong?" Tim suggested. "This might be the last time the four of us will get together for quite a while."

Danny saw the concern flash in Marilyn's eyes. "Well," she said reluctantly, "I think it would be all right."

"Is it your mom you're worried about, Marilyn?" Danny asked her.

She nodded. "She was sick this evening, you know. She complained about having a headache. She was going around in an old housecoat with her hair all stringy and everything."

"That wouldn't bother me any," Tim replied.

"I don't think we'd better," Danny and Kay said, almost together.

"Why don't we walk down by the lake?" Marilyn asked quickly. "It's too nice an evening to be in the house, anyway."

They walked across the street and up the narrow sidewalk toward the lake.

"Well," Kay said after they had walked a block or so, "it won't be long until I'll be heading home to Mexico."

"And I'll be going back to the Angle," Danny told her. "It's certainly going to be good to see that old lake again, and Jim and all my friends. A fellow really doesn't appreciate home until he's away, does he?"

"Are you going to write to me?" Kay asked.

He hesitated a moment. "Are you going to write to me?"

"If you write first."

"Don't worry about that," he. said, grinning. "I'll be writing. The only thing I'm going to miss about being here in Cedarton is getting to see you.

She stopped and turned to face him. "Or Marilyn," she added softly. The instant she spoke she stiffened and bit her lip. "I shouldn't have said that," she added.

He looked down at her. "Marilyn? Who said anything about Marilyn?"

"I shouldn't have said anything, Danny. I didn't mean to be catty, but—," her voice trailed away.

"But what?"

"You have been spending a lot of time over there lately," she finished, glad for the darkness that hid the flush in her cheeks.

Danny grinned. "She has a real nice Ping-Pong table." Then the smile left his face. "Seriously," he went on, "Marilyn's a nice girl and all that, but I'm certainly not interested in her. And she's not interested in me."

Kay was flustered momentarily. "Forgive me, Danny. I shouldn't have said anything. I've been a little jealous."

"I don't know of anyone else that I'd rather have interested in what I do, and whom I go with than you, Kay," he said a bit huskily.

* * *

Danny Orlis thought that they would all start back for the Angle the following day, but instead his mom and dad took the train for the Twin Cities.

"We've got some business to attend to," Mr. Orlis explained. "And while we're away we thought we'd go on down to Minneapolis for a few days."

"What about the twins, Dad?" Danny asked when the two of them were alone. "And that guy who was asking so many questions about them?"

"I don't think there's anything to worry about, Danny," Carl Orlis replied. "It must have been someone who remembered about the accident in which the twins' parents were killed and he got curious."

Danny said no more. Yet he was vaguely upset and disturbed as he left the depot alone.

There had been a picnic at the lake for the eighth grade that afternoon and neither Ron nor Roxie went to the depot with Danny. It was almost dark when they came running into the Meyers' house.

"Danny!" Ron cried. "Something terrible happened just now!"

Danny's face blanched. It had only been a year ago since Mr. Meyer's son had drowned at a school picnic on the same lake.

"He stopped us!" Roxie exclaimed, her lips trembling. "He stopped us right on Main Street on our way from the lake!"

"And do you know who it was?" Ron demanded, breaking in. "It was Uncle Harold!"

Harold Bauer! Danny sucked in his breath sharply. Harold Bauer had been the one who tried his best to get custody of the twins. That had happened back in Iron Mountain several years before, when he thought he could get his hands on the Bauer estate money.

"What did he want?" Danny tried to sound calm and assured, but his breath was coming in short gasps and the palms of his hands were moist with sweat.

"He asked us a whole bunch of questions," Ron said, the words tumbling out. "He wanted to know how we were being treated, what clothes we had, where we'd been going to school, and a lot of things like that, Danny."

Roxie shivered. "He said he wanted to find out if we were being taken care of properly. He said that if we weren't he was going to take us back to Colorado with him."

Danny put his arms about his adopted brother and sister. "You don't need to worry about that happening. I was talking with Dad this afternoon. He said that you are both legally adopted. You belong to Mom and Dad in the same way that I do. Neither your Uncle Harold, nor anyone else, can take you away from us."

Tears welled in Roxie's eyes. "Are you sure, Danny?" she repeated, her lips trembling. "Are you awfully sure?"

"Of course, I'm sure. One person can't come and take another person's children because they happen to feel like it."

Karen and Mrs. Meyer came into the room just then and Roxie went out into the kitchen with them.

"I'm sure Harold can't do anything legally, Ron," Danny said as soon as they were alone. "And I don't think he'd dare try anything else. But you and Roxie had better watch your step for the next two or three days, until the folks get back and we get home on the Angle."

Ron swallowed hard.

"And another thing," Danny said. "Don't go out on the streets after dark unless you're with me or Mr. and Mrs. Meyer. And whatever you do, don't leave Roxie, even for a minute."

Ron's face crinkled. "You mean I've got to take her with me when I go to say good-bye to all the gang?"

he asked. "And tag along with her when she goes to say good-bye to all those silly girls?"

"We've got to be awfully careful, Ron."

The next morning Danny was getting some of his things together so they could leave on short notice when Tim came over to see him.

"I got some news this morning," his friend said seriously.

"Good or bad?"

"That depends upon how you look at it," Tim said. "I got a letter from the coach at Crestwood. He wants me to be sure to come to Crestwood this fall as he has a part-time job for me."

THE VISITOR'S REASON

Danny and Tim were silent for a long while.

"Have you prayed about it?" Danny asked at last.

He flushed slightly. "I think God expects us to use our common sense, don't you, Danny?"

"Of course," Danny answered. "But He also expects us to call upon Him for guidance. How can we stay in the center of His will, Tim, unless we talk to Him about the problems we have to face?"

Tim Barton swallowed hard. "I – I'll try."

Danny closed his trunk and locked it.

"It's certainly good to see your mom coming to church regularly, Tim," the Orlis boy said, putting his laptop away and sitting down at the desk to face his friend.

Tim nodded. The smile came back to his lips." It's wonderful. And to think that she's a Christian now."

"I know how you feel," Danny answered.

* * *

There was choir practice at church that evening. When Marilyn got home about 9:30, she found her father sitting alone in the living room.

"Hi, Dad. Where's Mom?"

He closed the Bible he had been reading. "This is the evening her bridge club meets. She left right after dinner this evening."

Marilyn went to the divan and sat down across from him.

"Daddy," she said after a time, "what's the matter with Mom?"

"Why?"

"I don't know. Maybe it's just me, but it seems as though, lately, she's angry and upset all the time."

Harold Forester moistened his lips with the tip of his tongue. "I've noticed it too."

"I'd like to invite some of the kids over before they go back home," she said. "I'd like to have Kay and Danny, and Tim in for an evening, but I'm afraid to."

"I'm afraid your mother is very disappointed about the school you have decided to attend," he said thoughtfully.

"But I told her that I'd go to the U if she really wanted me to."

"You've been accepted at the Bible institute, and that's where I want you to go, at least for a couple of years."

Marilyn went over and sat on the arm of her dad's chair. "I wish there were some way we could get Mom to accept Christ as her Savior. That would solve all the problems."

He put his arm around her tenderly. "It might not solve all of them," he said. "But it would make it possible for them to be solved." He sighed deeply. "We don't want to give up hope or stop praying for her."

"Mom is at the very top of my prayer list."

"And Marilyn," he continued, "when your mom is cross and difficult with you, please be especially kind and understanding. She is finding all this as difficult as we are. And, in spite of the things she does sometimes, she loves us both very, very much."

Marilyn looked down at him. "I'll try awfully hard."

* * *

Kay had been in the choir, but now that she was leaving for Mexico at the end of the week, she had quit practicing with them. Danny came over to see her after dinner that evening and the two of them walked uptown.

"I wish Dad and Mom would get back from the Cities," Danny said later in the evening when they stopped at the cafe for a sandwich. "I'm getting awfully uneasy about having the twins down here. I don't trust that Harold Bauer."

* * *

Danny had been so busy the last few days of school that he hadn't had time to see the authorities out at the Bible institute. But now that he had his bags packed and his things in order, he went out to see Dr. Nielson.

"I'd like to get a line on what we'll be studying next fall," he said. "Especially the Bible subjects. I can do some special studying on them."

The superintendent took a sheet of paper from his desk and began to write down the subjects that Danny would have. "Tell me, Danny, what do you plan to do? What will your life work be?"

A question flickered on Danny's face. "I don't believe that I know what you mean."

"Have you felt any particular calling? Is the Lord directing you to the ministry, or the mission field, or some other field of Christian service?"

Danny Orlis pursed his lips.

"I don't know," he answered. "I haven't thought much about it. Guess I always figured that I'd just go back up on the Angle and raise a little garden, and trap and have some fishing cabins."

The superintendent looked thoughtful. "You should make this a definite matter of prayer, Danny," he said. "The Lord can use Christian farmers and business-men, of course. But, you know, He needs consecrated young men and women in His service too."

Danny was vaguely disturbed as he left the school and went back to the Meyer home. It was true that he had always thought he would get a little ground up by Pine Creek and do as his dad had done, but something was bothering him lately. He had noticed it whenever he had seen a young minister or read a missionary story – a longing, vague and indistinct, like the blur of mountains in the haze of early morning.

And with that longing was mixed resentment. After all, he told himself, he had been away from the Angle for four years going to school, and he would be away another four years finishing his education. The only thing that made the time away from home tolerable at all was the thought that one day he would be able to go back home and stay. After all, the Angle was his life. He could do what he wanted to. He could serve the Lord up there. They needed a good, solid Christian testimony among the people. That could be his field of service.

He walked slowly, the thoughts churning within his mind and heart.

By this time Danny Orlis had reached the block where the Meyer home stood. The house was dark except for a small light in the hall. He had started up the walk toward the porch when a car crept by with its lights out!

He sucked in his breath sharply. Quickly he dropped behind a bushy spirea. While he watched, the car made a U-turn and came back, inching along.

His heart was hammering madly. For an instant, his head swam! It was Harold Bauer! It had to be!

The car stopped directly in front of the house. "Danny!" an all too familiar voice called to him. "Danny Orlis! Is that you?"

That voice! It had been at least two years since he had heard it, but he would have recognized it any-where! It was Harold Bauer!

"Danny! Would you come here for a minute? I'd like to talk with you."

The car door opened, and Harold got out.

Danny straightened slowly and started toward him.

"I suppose the twins told you that I was in town."

Danny nodded without speaking.

"I've been wanting to talk to you."

He stood there waiting.

"You'll never know how much I've missed Ronald and Roxanne these past couple of years," Harold said.

The Orlis boy eyed him narrowly. He seemed serious enough. Yet—.

"They're the only blood relatives I have left in the world," he explained. "My other brother in California died about six months ago. The only family I have left is Ron and Roxie." He paused. "I know your parents can take care of them better than I ever could, but I just had to see them."

"I'm sure Dad and Mom wouldn't mind that."

Somehow, he felt sorry for the tall, dark-haired man. Harold Bauer seemed so lonesome and pathetic.

"I thought maybe if I could see your parents and talk with them," he continued, "I might persuade them to let me come up to the Lake of the Woods for a few days so I could get acquainted with the twins."

"You'll have to talk with Dad and Mom about that."

Harold laid his hand on Danny's arm. "You'll never know how much it would mean to me."

Danny stood there for a moment or two after Harold drove away. He had been so excited and had worried so terribly about the fact that Harold had come to Cedarton asking questions about Ron and Roxie. And all the while he only wanted to see them again.

CHAPTER 3

ANGLE INLET

In the Forester home, Marilyn and her father stood in the kitchen.

"Daddy," the girl said, "remember I said something about wanting to ask Kay, Tim, and Danny over for an evening before they go? Now the Orlises are back and they're all leaving the first thing in the morning. Would it be all right to have the kids in for a while this evening?"

"I don't see why not. But you'd better ask your mother first, to be sure that she doesn't have something planned."

After a short committee meeting at church Danny, Kay, and Tim went over to Marilyn's to spend the evening.

"When are you going to Mexico?" Tim asked Kay as they walked along the narrow sidewalk.

"I got a letter from Mom yesterday. She has to be at some sort of meeting in Mexico City for ten days, so I'm going to wait here until she's back. You see, she'll have to meet me at the bus stop about fifty miles from our station."

"I heard the most wonderful thing about your mom, Tim," Marilyn put in, stepping back on the porch so that he could open the screen door for her. "Isn't it wonderful to know that she's a Christian now?"

"I'll say it is," he answered. "It's hard to believe that it's really true. I've been praying and praying that she would be saved. It didn't seem as though she ever was going to take Christ as her Savior. Then, when I had almost given up hope and wasn't even expecting it, it happened."

"I'll certainly be happy when my mom does the same thing." Marilyn spoke sorrowfully.

The front door was unlocked and they went in. Mrs. Forester met them in the living room.

"Well!" she exclaimed. "Just what is this, Marilyn?"

"Don't you remember, Mom?" Marilyn asked. "I talked with you about having the kids in for the evening. Danny is leaving in the morning, and Kay will be going back to Mexico in a few days."

Mrs. Forester glared from one to another. "The least you could do, my dear, is have some respect for your poor mother. Or didn't you know that my head has been splitting all day?"

"That's too bad," Kay said quickly, concern in her voice. "We don't want to bother you if you're sick."

"I insist that you stay," Mrs. Forester continued

acidly. "Marilyn has invited you. And we always want her guests to feel welcome."

"But you're sick, Mrs. Forester," Danny said. "We can come over another time."

"I insist," she retorted sharply. "Go down in the basement and have a good time. Make as much noise as you wish. Don't bother about me."

Tim started to speak, but she cut him off.

"When you're finished," Mrs. Forester continued, "I'm sure you can find something to eat in the icebox. If you'll call me, I'll be glad to get up and fix lunch for you."

With that, she turned and almost staggered up the stairs.

For a moment or two Marilyn could not speak. Tears filled her eyes.

"I think we'd better go," Tim said uncertainly. "We can come back again sometime when your mom is feeling better."

"But – ," Marilyn stopped and swallowed hard. "Danny and Kay will both be gone," she blurted. "I'll go up and talk, with Mom. Wait for me until I get back."

For several minutes Danny, Kay, and Tim stood there in embarrassment. Finally, Marilyn came slowly down the stairs.

"I don't think we'd better stay, Marilyn," Kay said. "Your mom doesn't feel well, and we might disturb her."

"I – I suppose it would be best." She was swallowing hard.

They went silently out of the house and down the street to a clean little cafe.

"I don't understand it," Marilyn said after they had placed their orders. "I talked with her this morning about having you over. She even helped me fix the sandwiches."

"Perhaps she got to feeling so bad that she felt she just couldn't have company," Kay said.

Marilyn looked up at her quickly. "I—," she began, but stopped suddenly. "If she did," she went on lamely, "she didn't say anything about it.'

They were still sitting in the booth talking when Mr. Forester came in.

"Oh, there you are," he said, going up to the booth where they were sitting. "I wish I'd been home a few minutes ago." He pulled up a chair at the end of the booth and sat down. "I think it would have been all right for you to have stayed. But keep praying for Mrs. Forester. She must be under conviction, or she wouldn't do these things."

"We didn't mean to bother her," Danny said quickly.

Mr. Forester shook his head. He ordered a sandwich and a cup of coffee, then turned back to the young people.

"I came to tell you about something," he said. "I hope none of you has any plans for the next week or ten days."

"Why, Daddy?" Marilyn asked him.

"For several days I have been talking with Mom," he said. "Do you remember that Bible camp I was telling you about, Marilyn? The one that's on an island in the Lake of the Woods not too far from where Danny lives?"

"I know where that is," Danny put in. "I was there once last summer. It's up in Monument Bay."

"I've been talking with Mrs. Forester about it," he went on. "She has finally agreed to go up there with us. I thought perhaps the rest of you would like to go too."

"Do you really mean that?" Tim echoed, as though he could scarcely believe it.

"Of course, there's a catch to it," he told them. "My sister's boys are going to come here in the next couple of days to spend some time with us. I've been concerned about their salvation. I've tried to write to them and their mother about the Lord, but I haven't been able to get very far with them. I thought maybe if we all went up to camp for a couple of weeks, they would accept Christ while we are there."

"That sounds swell," Danny said exuberantly. "You'll get in some good fishing too. Monument Bay is one of the best sections of the Lake of the Woods when it comes to muskie fishing."

* * *

The following day Danny, the twins, and his parents got on the bus and went back to Warroad to take the boat out to Angle Inlet. Danny's friend, Jim, was waiting for him at the bus depot.

"Hi, Danny," he exclaimed, shaking the Orlis boy's hand vigorously. "It's sure good to see you again."

Danny looked about the friendly little town. "It's good to be back again, Jim. How are things up on the Angle?"

"I was up there yesterday," Jim answered. "The fish are really biting."

Danny grinned.

"There's a friend of yours over on Bear River. Danny," Jim went on. "He—

"A friend of mine?" Danny cut in.

"That's what he said," Jim replied. "He flew in this morning. Wanted us to take him out on the boat, but when he found out that he'd have to wait until tomorrow he hired a plane to fly him up. He seemed to be in an awful hurry."

Danny scratched his head. There was only one guy he could think of who had said anything about visiting them. But why would Harold Bauer have gone on ahead? Did he have a reason for wanting to get up on the Angle before Danny and his parents got back?

Danny pushed his hat back on his head and stared thoughtfully out across the Big Traverse. For some reason that old uneasy feeling had come back.

CHAPTER 4

A CHARGE TO DANNY

Danny Orlis and his dad stood on the dock in front of their cabins on Pine Creek and looked across the bay toward Big McCoy Island.

"Why would Harold Bauer be in such a hurry to get up here, Dad?"

Mr. Orlis turned to watch a seagull spread its wings and soar in a big, graceful circle above them. "I've been wondering that myself."

Harold Bauer was nice enough. He had taken a room with one of the Orlises' neighbors on Bear River and came over to see the twins as often as possible. He was a good fisherman and he and the twins spent a great deal of time on the lake.

"Boy, Danny," Ron exclaimed as they came in with their limit catch of walleyes, "you should have been with us this afternoon!"

Harold looped his arm around Ron's shoulder.

"Yes, sir, Danny," he said, smiling. "Ron is getting to be quite a fisherman. If he were living with me, we'd have some big times together."

Danny eyed him narrowly.

When Danny went to bed that night, he was still vaguely disturbed. It wasn't anything positive, anything that he could tell his dad about. Instead, it was more of a feeling, like you get when someone behind is staring at you. Only this left a lump of ice in his stomach. The feeling was still with him the next morning but began to melt a little when he met Harold later and the Harold made a great show of friendliness.

"I only hope I'm not annoying your parents, Danny," he said seriously. "I'm enjoying the twins so much that sometimes I don't think about anyone else."

Danny told his dad about it.

"I'm glad to know that, Danny," Carl Orlis answered. "I hate to be suspicious and critical, but I couldn't help wondering about Harold."

"Do you think you'll be able to spare me for a few days?" Danny asked. "I'd like to go over to the Broken Arrow Bible Camp for a week or so while Kay, the Foresters, and Tim are over there."

His dad eyed him quizzically. Danny felt the color come up in his cheeks.

"I guess it'll be all right," Mr. Orlis told him.

Early the next morning Danny took his little boat, the *Scappoose,* and went racing over the mirror-like water toward Monument Bay and the Broken Arrow

Bible Camp. He got there an hour or so before the packet boat from Warroad arrived with the Foresters and their guests.

Danny shook hands with Bob and Harry, Marilyn's cousins, and then shoved his way past the others to get to Kay.

"Hi," he said, reaching for her bag.

She smiled up at him. "I can carry that, Danny," she answered, "but if you want to help me you can get some of my other things out of the boat."

"Sure thing," he answered, turning toward the lower deck where the freight was piled. A moment later he stuck his head up the stairway. "Hey," he called, "all I can find down here is an English saddle and some riding gear."

"That's it."

"What gives? What do you plan on doing with that stuff?"

"Didn't I tell you?" she asked him. "I'm going to teach some advanced riding classes up here."

Danny pushed his hat back on his forehead and ran his fingers through his sandy hair. "You teach riding?" he echoed.

"Would you like to take a few lessons?" she said laughing. The two of them walked off the dock and up the rocky slope to the cabin where Kay and Marilyn were to stay.

"I still don't get this horse riding business," he continued. "I could see Marilyn doing it, maybe, but you—," he stopped lamely, shaking his head.

For a brief instant, her face flushed. "Mother paid her way through school teaching advanced riding and jumping," she said. "I've been riding ever since I could walk."

Danny Orlis looked at her with new admiration. Now that she spoke of it, he remembered that first time he met her when he and Jim went to Mexico. She had ridden like an Indian then, bareback or in a saddle.

They had a campfire service that night and the speaker spoke on sin. Mrs. Forester came to the meeting and sat with her husband, a little to one side of the others as though she wanted to make it clear that she was not one of them.

"We all need a Savior," the speaker said. " 'For all have sinned and come short of the glory of God.' The day is coming when we will have to pay the penalty for our sins. The day is coming when we will have to make a decision concerning Christ. We will have to acknowledge that Jesus is the Son of God. We can either acknowledge Him in this life where there is an opportunity for repentance, or we must acknowledge Him in the next life where there will be opportunity only for judgment and regret….

Mrs. Forester bit her lower lip. Her face was pale and drawn, and her eyes hollow and ringed with dark circles. Suddenly she looked very old, far beyond her years.

Danny glanced her way and saw that she squirmed nervously. Without taking his eyes off the speaker he began to pray for her, silently. He asked God to bring conviction to her heart, to lead her to repentance and an acceptance of the Lord Jesus as her personal Savior.

By this time, the message was over.

"I don't usually ask for a show of hands," the speaker said, "but somehow, I feel led to do so tonight. I want to give you an opportunity to take Christ as your Savior if you have not already done so."

Mrs. Forester stared at him with grim determination darkening her face. His words made her uneasy. For the first time a desperate, unnamed longing welled within her.

But they weren't going to make a fool out of her. She'd get her mind on something else. That was it! She wouldn't even listen to him. She'd think about the clothes she'd have to help Marilyn get ready for school. She'd think about her trip back to Cedarton, which couldn't come any too soon. Perhaps she'd even go on down to the Cities with a couple of the women in her set to take in a show and do the stores.

But, think about it or not, she felt her whole being turn to ice. Her husband must have noticed. She could feel him watching her. Suddenly she was furious at him.

Why did he bring her here in the first place? He knew that her life was good enough. He knew that she didn't go for this fanatical religion that had taken hold of him and Marilyn and was ruining all their lives. What was the matter with him?

The group was standing now, heads bowed, singing the last verse of an invitation song. She twisted her handkerchief into a tight little knot. As they began the chorus Mr. Forester turned gently to her.

"Carrie," he almost whispered, "wouldn't you like to settle things with God now?"

He had spoken as gently as he ever had, but she looked up at him, her eyes blazing. For a brief instant, she tried to speak. Then that blank, wild stare came into her eyes. She gave a deep little moan and crumpled beside him.

Danny and Tim helped Mr. Forester stretch her out on the seats. The doctor came over quickly and checked her pulse.

"Her heart seems to be all right," he said. "It could be that she got a little warm out here this evening."

Harold Forester took her hand in his own. "I'm afraid that Carrie doesn't need a doctor," he said sorrowfully, "for her body, I mean. It's her soul that's sick."

He felt her body stiffen as he spoke.

She opened her eyes presently, allowed herself to be helped to her feet, and walked uncertainly toward their cabin.

"Do you feel better, Carrie?"

She glared at him. "I've never been so humiliated in my life."

The next morning Danny and Tim were on their way to breakfast when Mr. Orlis came roaring up to the dock in his fast boat.

"Look," Danny exclaimed, "there's Dad! I wonder what brought him over here!"

He and his friend dashed to the dock, reaching it almost at the same time as Carl Orlis glided in.

"What's wrong, Dad?" Danny demanded excitedly. "What's the matter?"

Carl Orlis threw a light line about the nearest post and snubbed his boat to it.

"I found out something, Danny," he said seriously, in a tone his son had never heard him use before; "it explains everything about Harold Bauer."

"What do you mean, Dad?" Danny demanded.

"Last night the sheriff flew here, with a subpoena for me. Harold is suing for Ron and Roxie!"

Danny felt his face drain white. A big lump choked in his throat. "But how?" he managed weakly. "We adopted them legally and everything, didn't we?"

Mr. Orlis nodded. "Harold claims that the judge who awarded the twins to us hadn't given proper notice of the hearing in Colorado. He says that he didn't know about it in time to prepare his own claim for the twins."

"But he did, Dad," Danny protested. "He was right in the courtroom."

"That's what your mother said," Mr. Orlis answered. "But the question is, does the court record note that fact? And even if it does, does that prove he had time to present his claim for the children?"

"You don't think he can take them away from us, do you, Dad?"

"We'll have to go to court to find out," Carl Orlis told him. "But that isn't the only thing that's worrying me."

Danny said nothing.

"In a case like this," Mr. Orlis went on, "having possession of the children means so much, I'm afraid he might try to kidnap them!"

"He wouldn't dare!"

"That guy would do anything, Danny. That's why I came to see you. I want you to look after the twins for us over here until we get this thing straightened out!"

Danny bit his lower lip. "But what if Harold –" his voice trailed away.

CHAPTER 5

A THRILLING RESCUE

That very afternoon Carl Orlis came back to the Bible Camp with Ron and Roxie.

"I didn't expect you so soon, Dad," Danny told him.

"I did plan to wait until tomorrow, Danny, but your mother thought it would be better to get the twins over here right away."

"I still don't see how he can do anything," the Orlis boy answered. "We went through court to get the twins, and they've lived with us all this time."

"The law is strange sometimes," his dad said. "For example, having possession of the kids in a case like this can make a great deal of difference. That's why it's so important for you to keep a close watch on them."

Danny stopped at the door of the cabin where Roxie would be staying. "You won't need to worry, Dad," he said seriously. "I'll keep my eye on them every minute."

"I know you will," Carl Orlis answered.

He left then and Danny turned from the dock and started up the narrow path. Ron came to meet him.

"How come we have to stay over here, Danny?" he demanded belligerently. "We haven't been home since the second semester started, and now the folks cart us over here and dump us. What's the big idea?"

"Dad and Mom thought it would be best," Danny told him. "Dad explained about that lawsuit your Uncle Harold is bringing to get custody of you and Roxie. He thought it would be better to have you here until your uncle leaves the Angle."

"I don't think he'd do anything," Ron said defensively. "He's a swell guy. The trouble is that you and Dad have it in for him."

Danny stared at his younger brother. "He has tried already, Ron," he said. "The sheriff was out and served the papers just yesterday."

"I don't care," the younger boy retorted hotly. "If he did, there must be some reason for it. Uncle Harold's a swell guy." With that, he turned and strode away.

Danny stared after him. A few weeks before, Ron had been able to see Harold Bauer for what he was. He distrusted him instinctively. But now – Danny pushed his cap back on his head and ran his fingers through his tousled hair.

The next morning dawned clear and calm. But within an hour the wind began to build. And by the time the breakfast bell sounded it was whipping in a howling crescendo out of the Northwest, sweeping the full length of the largest expanse of water near the camp. Long, deep-rolling breakers raced across the shallow water to dash spray high above the dock and slam resoundingly against the rocks on shore.

Danny and Tim stood for a moment and watched it on their way to breakfast.

"Well," Danny observed, "no fishing today."

Later that morning Mr. Forester sought Danny out.

"Danny," he said breathlessly, "have you seen Harry and Bill?"

Danny noticed the concern in Mr. Forester's eyes. "Why, no, not recently."

"I saw them about a half hour ago," Tim said. "They were complaining about the fishing expedition being called off."

Fear flashed across Mr. Forester's face. "There's a boat missing," he said as his voice trailed away miserably.

"You don't suppose they're out on that rough water, do you?" Danny asked as though he could not believe it. "Even an experienced fisherman wouldn't go out on a day like this."

He stared across the foam-laced lake. Harry and Bill wouldn't have dared to go out on the water with the wind raging that way – or would they?

Danny and Mr. Forester turned, almost at the same time, and started on the run toward the dock. By the time they reached it forty or fifty kids had gathered on the shore.

"Look!" one of them shouted. "The motor on that boat is running and there's nobody in it!"

The color drained from Danny's face. His heart stood still. There was a boat out there, lurching dangerously from one wave to another. It turned haphazardly to roll with the seas and took water over the side.

"That's a Broken Arrow boat!" Mr. Forester cried hoarsely. "It must be the one Harry and Bill took!"

For a brief instant, Danny stared at the wildly careening boat. The motor was racing at full throttle, driving the light aluminum craft into the breakers with such force that it showered spray in a great white plume on each side.

"They've been thrown out!" Harold Forester exclaimed, gasping. Cold beads of perspiration pearled his forehead, only to be whipped away by the driving wind.

Mrs. Forester, who had come up beside her husband, screamed hysterically.

"What have you done to them, Harold?" she cried. "What have you done to them?"

He put his arm about her, but for a moment could not speak.

"If it weren't for that fanatical religion of yours," she shrilled, "this wouldn't have happened! You've driven the boys to it! That's what you've done!"

The boat made a wide, sweeping circle, lurching violently as it came about. Danny sucked in his breath sharply. He had seen boats upset with less reason than that. His heart hammered against his ribs.

Dimly, as though she were far away, he heard Mrs. Forester lash out at her husband again. "I've told you and told you that you'd only cause trouble trying to get everyone to believe that fanatical religion of yours!" Her voice rose dangerously. "Now you've gotten Harry and Billy so worked up about it that they've gone out in a storm and – and drowned! I hope you're satisfied."

She only stopped for breath, but Danny wasn't listening anymore. For an empty aluminum boat, that one was riding awfully low in the water. And why did it continue to circle and turn so smoothly? Unless – in that instant the answer came to him. He began to rip off his shoes.

"What are you going to do?" Harold Forester demanded.

Without waiting to explain Danny jerked off his shirt and dove into the water swimming against the battering breakers out to the camp launch which was anchored a hundred yards or so offshore. There was a prayer in every breath, in every heartbeat, in every long, powerful stroke of his arms.

If what he suspected were true, he dared not waste an instant in getting out to the wildly racing boat.

In half a minute he reached the launch, hoisted himself over the side and without waiting to catch his breath, loosed the mooring lines and dove for the starter. The big motor came to life with a roar, but not before the driving wind had swept the launch halfway to shore.

The runaway boat was half a block from him now, swinging away in a great arc.

Cautiously he opened the throttle on the big marine engine. The launch thrust her nose in the air as her propeller blades bit into the water. A moment later the nose dropped as she began to plane, almost leaping from one wave to the next.

Danny resisted an almost uncontrollable urge to cut the speed. A boat could plow her nose into a wave and upend in seas like that. But he dared not do it the safe way. There wasn't time!

It seemed as though all the camp had lined up on shore and were watching breathlessly, prayerfully. He caught a glimpse of them as he edged the launch about to head straight for the speeding outboard.

Without warning the boat ahead whirled so fast that for a brief instant, it hung precariously on the crest of a wave, shuddering under the impact and lurching with wild abandon. Then the runaway came about and headed straight toward the launch, riding in the teeth of the wind!

Danny saw what was happening and turned the wheel hard. The launch responded sluggishly and rolled so violently that Danny caught his breath and grasped involuntarily for the top edge of the side of the boat with one hand. With the other, he jerked the wheel back and the launch hesitated uncertainly!

The two boats were scarcely ten feet apart, headed straight toward one another! There was no time to turn, no time to cut the speed! The two boats crashed together, head-on! The nose of the aluminum boat crumpled like paper, and she tipped over as a big wave broke over her.

There was a scream of terror from the other boat! Harry and Bill had been in the other boat all the time, crouching on the floor and enjoying the excitement they were causing. Now Danny heard their screams of terror and saw them go sprawling into the water.

"O heavenly Father," he prayed as the launch swept within inches of the boys and went on past, "help me to get to them."

Hurriedly he brought the launch about and headed back, cutting the throttle as he did so.

One of the boys came up, thrashing wildly with his arms. An instant later the other head appeared beside him.

Danny never did remember just how he managed to get both of the boys out of the water. He recalled throwing the life preserver toward them. He remembered how they clung to one another, ignoring the life ring until he dove into the water and with a savage blow knocked Bill away from his brother. He remembered holding Bill and treading water while Mr. Forester and the camp director pulled Harry into another boat and came over to take Bill. He remembered standing on the dock, numb with fear, while the director and a counselor administered artificial respiration.

"Is he going to be all right?" Harry asked, his voice quivering.

"It's going to be a real miracle if he is."

Harry's lower lip was trembling. "It was all my fault," he managed. "I thought of the scheme. I thought it would be fun to get everybody excited. Then we were going to stand up and have the laugh on everybody." He swallowed hard and would have continued, but he could not.

Danny came over and took him by the arm.

"Come on," he said softly. "Let's go over here where you can lie down for a minute or two."

"If something happens to Bill," Harry continued, "it's all my fault. I've caused it all."

Nevertheless, he allowed himself to be guided off the dock and up the path toward the nearest cabin.

With his hand on the cabin door, Danny stopped. "I think there's someone in there, Harry," he said. "Perhaps we'd better go to the next cabin."

He started to turn, but Harry did not move. "Listen."

He and Danny stood silently outside the door.

"What are they doing in there?" he demanded. "They're talking about Bill and me!"

Danny pushed the door open slightly.

"O heavenly Father," they heard Kay praying, "just be with Bill, don't let him die now. He doesn't know You as Savior, Lord. Help him to get well so he will have another chance to confess his sin and put his trust in You...."

Harry Winston grasped Danny by the arm. His fingers bit into Danny's biceps until the cords stood out on the backs of his hands.

Kay stopped then and Tim began, praying earnestly for the unconscious boy.

"Danny," Harry said, hoarsely. "I don't know Jesus as my Savior, either!"

"You can take care of that, fellow," the young woodsman said softly.

Harry was silent.

"All you have to do is to recognize that you're a sinner and put your trust in Jesus. It's the simplest thing in the world."

Together they knelt outside the cabin door, and Danny guided Harry Winston as he prayed his first stumbling prayer of confession.

Neither of the boys heard the footsteps approach them. But when they finally finished praying and got slowly to their feet, Mr. Forester was standing there.

"Harry," he said, his voice hushed. "Bill wants to talk to you."

"Bill?" Harry echoed. "Is he – is he – ?" But he had no need to ask. The answer was written in the happiness on Mr. Forester's face. He choked suddenly and could say no more.

"He wants to talk to you," Mr. Forester repeated.

Harry smiled faintly. "I want to talk to him too," he said. "I want to talk to him about the most important thing I've ever done!"

CHAPTER 6

THE LETTER FROM MEXICO

Danny had hoped to see a great deal of Kay during the two weeks they were to be at Broken Arrow. But she had been so busy teaching horsemanship and her advanced riding classes that he scarcely got to see her at all, except during and right after the meetings.

He went over to watch her and stood admiringly on the sidelines while she put a big, nervous black over the jumps.

"I want you to watch the way I lean forward and help the horse over the jump," she explained to her students, swinging easily into the saddle. "Remember, your horse wants to do what you want him to do, but you've got to make your wish clear to him. And, above all, he wants to feel your confidence. If you go into the jump uncertainly, your horse will falter every time."

"That gal can really handle a horse," somebody beside Danny said.

He turned a little to see Chuck Martin, a handsome young college fellow, who had come to camp a few days before to spend the balance of the summer.

"Yes, sir," Chuck went on admiringly. "I'm going to have to get acquainted with her."

Danny waited until Kay finished her hour of instruction and helped her put her riding equipment away.

"I didn't know you could ride like that," he told her. They walked along the beach and out on the dock together.

"I've been doing that since I was knee-high," she said offhandedly.

"But you don't act a bit afraid."

She glanced at him queerly. "What is there to be afraid of?" she asked. "If you know how to handle a horse, he isn't going to hurt you."

A big mallard drake circled gracefully above them and for two or three minutes they watched it silently.

"I can't help wishing that I was down home," she said after a time. "You know, it's been nine whole months since I've seen Mom."

"It must be tough being a missionary's kid, at that."

She was silent, and Danny thought he saw the faintest glint of bitterness in her eyes.

"It is hard, Danny," she answered truthfully. "Sometimes I get to feeling as though it just isn't fair to have to be away from the people I love the most."

That evening the two of them went to the meeting together. Tim was already there, but the singing was almost over before Marilyn came hurrying in.

"We were beginning to wonder what happened to you," Kay whispered softly.

"It was Mom," she whispered back. "She had another sick spell this evening just as we were getting ready to come over here."

"Did you call the doctor?"

Marilyn shook her head. "No," she said, "but Daddy stayed with her."

Danny Orlis took a deep breath. It had been that way so often the past three or four days. Mrs. Forester had a sick headache when it came time to attend a service, or she was sleepy, or she had to write a letter, or wash out a few things.

"I'd certainly like to have you boys pray for us," Marilyn's dad had said to Danny and Tim only that morning. "My wife must be greatly under conviction. She's got a dozen excuses to keep from attending the services."

Marilyn too asked them to pray for her mom that evening when the meeting was over.

"Somehow," she said seriously, "I feel that if Mom leaves here without taking Christ as her Savior, she might never do it."

"We must put our trust in Him," Kay answered.

"I keep telling myself that," Marilyn replied. "But it's so hard."

When Danny and Kay reached the door to Kay's cabin she turned. "It was a nice evening," she told him, smiling warmly.

For an instant he said nothing. As he started to speak, he caught sight of an envelope stuck in the door.

"Say," he exclaimed, taking hold of it. "What's this?"

Kay glanced at the handwriting in the bright moonlight. "Why, it's a letter from Mom," she answered. "I've been wondering why I haven't heard from her."

Stepping inside the little porch she switched on the light and tore the envelope open hurriedly.

"I'll be seeing you in the morning," Danny said, starting to leave.

He was on the step when she called to him. "Wait, Danny!" she cried. "Wait, please!"

He came back instantly to see that her face was white and drawn and her lips were trembling.

"What's wrong?" he asked her.

She was still staring at the letter in her hand, still reading with tear-blurred eyes.

For a moment she could not answer him. Her fingers were trembling.

"What's happened, Kay?" he insisted. "Is she sick?"

"It isn't that. She's all right."

"What is it then?"

She tried to speak, but swallowed hard and shook her head. A tear escaped from under her eyelids and coursed, unheeded, down her cheek. Wordlessly she handed him the letter.

I don't know just how to write this, Kay, darling. I've been waiting and waiting in the hopes that I wouldn't have to write it at all. But I don't think it's fair to you to put it off any longer.

I know how your heart is set on going to Bible school. I'm sure you know that I'm just as anxious for it as you are. But Kay, we got word about two weeks ago that the church that has been paying for your support had a drop in missionary offerings during the past six months. And at the last business meeting the congregation voted to cut their share of your support in half. I've gone over the problem with the Superintendent down here, and with the men in the States, but they don't seem to have any ready answer. I plan to help all I can, of course, but even though you had gotten your full support, Bible school would have taken all the money I would have been able to spare to help you....

There was more to the letter, but Danny didn't read it. For some reason, the words had blurred and were starting to swim before his eyes.

CHAPTER 7

HAROLD BAUER RETURNS

For a long minute Danny and Kay stood there, staring at one another.

"That's tough, Kay," Danny said lamely.

"That means I – I won't be able to go to Bible school this fall, Danny," she said, fumbling for words. "And I've been counting on it so very much."

"I know just how you feel," he told her. "But, Kay, we still have the Lord. He supplied your support in the first place. He'll be able to raise up someone to take on the responsibility for your needs again. This may just be a time of testing."

"Testing!" she exclaimed bitterly. "That's all my life has been! A time of testing!"

The sudden anger in her voice startled him.

"It isn't fair, Danny! It isn't fair! My daddy was killed down in Mexico. Mom and I have had to live there alone. That is, when I could be down there with her. I've had to spend most of the time in boarding schools and with relatives or anyone who was willing to look out for me. When I was with Mom, I didn't have any other American children to play with. And when I was back in the States, I had to be away from her. I don't know what God expects! My whole life has been a sacrifice!"

With that she burst into tears and, turning, she ran into the cabin and slammed the door.

Danny Orlis stood there a few moments. The sudden outburst had almost taken his breath away. Quiet, gentle, little Kay! He had never thought such bitterness and anger could be bottled up within her. He took a step or two, uncertainly, toward the door, then paused. Marilyn and Tim came up just then. He told them what had happened.

"Oh, poor Kay," Marilyn's eyes filled with tears. "I'll go in and talk with her."

"She needs someone awfully bad right now."

He went back to his cabin after a time, but try as he would, he could not get to sleep. It was easy enough to tell Kay to trust in the Lord, to tell her that she should pray for help, to go ahead with her plans and to depend upon God to supply her needs. That sort of thing made good sermons, but it was harder to do than it sounded. And all because people back home had neglected to give.

The missionaries made the sacrifices of leaving loved ones, modern conveniences, and opportunities to get ahead. The least those Christians who remained at home could do would be to remain faithful in giving. Danny swung his feet over the side of the bunk and sat up. He had been so concerned about his own schooling that even he had been neglecting to give his tithe to the Lord in recent weeks!

The next morning Kay's face was a mask as she came to breakfast. She smiled woodenly and laughed at the jokes that were told at the table, trying hard to make everyone feel there was nothing wrong. She would have succeeded too had it not been for that bleak, cold look in her eyes.

"How do you feel?" Danny asked her softly.

She shook her head. For a brief instant, the smile fled from her face. *

"I want you to know," he told her, "that we're all praying for you."

She smiled her thanks.

That morning when she went out to teach her riding class, Chuck Martin came over to the stable.

"Can I help you saddle up?" he asked her.

"I can manage, thank you."

"I'll say you can. You're one of the best horsemen I've ever seen. How about the two of us going riding sometime?"

He got the bridle from its peg in the tack room and put it on the horse she planned to use that morning.

"I've done a lot of riding myself, but I don't know if I'll ever be able to do some of the things you've been demonstrating."

Kay liked the big, friendly guy and when the riding class was over, the two of them sat on the corral fence talking like old friends. She had only known him for half an hour but found herself telling him what had happened in regard to her going away to school.

"That's really tough," he said. "From where I sit it looks as though it's too much to ask of anybody."

"I wouldn't say that," she answered defensively. "Missionaries know what they're going into when they go out to the foreign field. They don't do it because it's easy, or because they make a lot of money. They do it so they can take the Gospel of the Lord Jesus Christ to people who would never hear it otherwise."

"I know all that, but it's the kids I'm thinking of. They're the ones who have to make the big sacrifices. Now take yourself, for instance. You didn't have anything at all to do with your parents' going down to Mexico. But you've had to live with a bunch of natives until you were old enough to go to school. Then you had to be away from your parents. I don't think it's fair!"

Kay was silent. "Serving the Lord is never easy."

"It isn't that I think we should let those people go on their pagan way," Chuck continued. "I'm as interested in seeing souls won as the next one. But I just can't see making other people suffer, and especially your own loved ones, in order to do it."

"I get along," she retorted tartly.

"I suppose a lot of people would be shocked to know that I feel as I do," Chuck said. He was silent for a time and his face grew dark. "I wasn't going to tell you this, Kay, but I'm a missionary kid myself. My parents are in Borneo now. I haven't seen them for three years and haven't lived with them for fifteen. Sometimes I cringe inside when I hear people talk about how wonderful it must be to have your parents out helping to win the heathen. I don't even know my own dad."

His face was set, and bitterness curled his lips and put a gleam in his eyes. "I can tell you this much," he continued, "they're not going to be able to get me out to the mission field or anywhere else where my family will have to make the sacrifices that I have."

"You mustn't feel that way, Chuck," Kay protested. "If we love the Lord, we've got to do what He wants us to."

Chuck Martin grinned crookedly at her. "I love the Lord, all right. I settled that a long time ago. But I'm going to remain the master of my life. I'm not going to ruin it the way my parents did theirs." He stopped uncertainly, and for a time a heavy silence hung between them.

A week ago, twenty-four hours ago, Kay would have had the answer to his bitterness. But now – she paused. She knew what the answers should be. But did she really believe them? Were they actually true? There had been times when she had felt injured and neglected in the past. But for the first time the same deep-seated, bitter anger that had warped Chuck's life and outlook began to take hold of her.

Danny Orlis finished his work at the camp early and hurried over to the riding stable to spend a few minutes with Kay before the next meeting started. When he got there, she and Chuck had just jumped off the fence and were standing beside the gate, talking.

"I'll take a rain check on that ride, Kay," Martin was saying.

"Sounds good to me. Tomorrow?"

Danny couldn't account for the sudden chill that took hold of his heart.

* * *

One of the Mounties who had eaten dinner that noon with the Orlises at Angle Inlet stopped in at the Bible camp that evening with a letter for Danny.

"I saw your dad today. He asked me to deliver this letter to you. Said to tell you that it's mighty important."

"Thanks," Danny replied, taking the big envelope and opening it. Roxie came up just then.

"Did you get a letter from Mom and Dad, Danny?" she asked. "What did they say?"

He reached over and rumpled her hair. "Now you just give me a minute to read it," he answered, "and I'll tell you what it said."

"I hope they're all right," his sister went on. "I've been so worried about them. Mom's looked terribly tired and worn out the past couple of weeks."

Danny nodded.

> I was in town and talked with our lawyer yesterday, Danny. Frankly, it doesn't look too good. He said we would have a tough battle if Harold actually takes this thing to court.

There was more about the lawyer's plans to keep the twins out of Harold's hands, and a list of questions which he wanted Danny to answer immediately. His dad went on:

> And, Danny, whatever you do, keep a close watch on Ron and Roxie. Harold Bauer is in the area again. And Mr. Pratt said that if he should manage to get possession of the children and get them up into Canada, it could be awfully hard for us to get them back. I think I explained the problem of extradition to you….

Danny read the letter over again, biting his lower lip thoughtfully.

"Is everything all right at home?" Roxie asked, pressing close to Danny and reaching for the letter.

"Mom and Dad are both well." He folded the letter and put it in his pocket.

"Can't I read it?" she asked almost plaintively. "I'm so lonesome for Mom."

"I don't think you'd better read this one," he said. "But everything is all right at home, Roxie. You can be sure of that."

"Then why can't I read the letter? You've always let me read the others."

"I know," he said as gently as possible, "but I don't think you'd better read this one."

Ron came running up just then.

"Roxie!" he cried. "I'll bet you can't guess who I just saw!"

She turned to face him.

"Uncle Harold!" Ron exclaimed. "He just stopped at the dock in his boat and is coming up the path!"

CHAPTER 8

A QUESTION FOR RON

L et's go down to the dock to meet him," Ron exclaimed excitedly.

She looked at Danny. "Is it all right?"

He nodded numbly and followed the twins down to the dock.

The older man threw his arm around Ron with exaggerated friendliness and smiled warmly at Roxie.

"I had an awful time finding you two," he said. "Mr. Orlis wouldn't tell me where you were. I had to go to one of the neighbors."

"I didn't want to leave," Ron told him. "But Dad made me."

"I can't understand that. I told Mr. Orlis I was only going to be gone for a few days, and then I was coming back so you and I could make that fishing trip we've been planning."

Ron's face lighted.

"Do you mean that we're still going to get to go?"

"Sure thing. I've chartered a plane and everything. We'll leave the first thing in the morning."

"Boy, that'll be swell," Ron said. "Are the fish really as big up there as everybody says?"

"I never saw such big lake trout in all my life. And northern pike! Why, we've pulled them out until our arms got tired."

"Did you hear that, Danny?" Ron asked.

Harold Bauer looked over at Danny. His eyes narrowed, and the corners of his mouth drew down to a thin, hard line. "Do you suppose you could find me a place to stay and something to eat, Orlis?"

"You can check with Mr. Harmon, the camp director," Danny told him.

Harold Bauer went to see the camp director about a cabin, but there was a new group of youngsters expected that afternoon, and there was no extra room for him.

"I imagine the best you'll be able to do," Mr. Harmon said, "is to get a room at Penasse."

"Did young Orlis come and talk to you about not letting me stay here?" Harold Bauer demanded sarcastically.

"Of course not."

"Don't give me that."

He swaggered down to the dock and got into his boat. Danny followed him.

"I'll be back after Ron in the morning."

"You won't need to," Danny told him. "He isn't going with you."

"What do you mean?"

"Dad gave me instructions not to let either Ron or Roxie go anywhere. They've got to stay here."

"What's the matter? Are you afraid I'll run off with them?"

"You'll have to talk with Dad about his reasons. But he told me not to let either of the twins go any-where with you, not even for five minutes."

"Ron's going to be mighty disappointed about missing that fishing trip."

"There will be plenty of time for Ron to go fishing later," Danny said.

Harold Bauer opened the gas valve on his outboard motor and turned back to the young woodsman.

"I've decided that I want those twins, and I'm going to get them," he said gritting his teeth. "One way or another!"

With that, he jerked hard on the starter rope and his big motor started with a roar.

Ron came down to the dock just in time to see him head out of the bay and beyond the long finger of land that blotted him from view.

"Where did Uncle Harold go?"

"I don't know, Ron. I told him that Dad didn't want you or Roxie to go anywhere with him, so he left. I don't believe he'll be back."

Disappointment flashed across the younger boy's

face. "You mean that I – I can't go on that fishing trip with him?"

"Dad said you weren't to go anywhere with your Uncle Harold."

"But Danny! He's my uncle!"

Ron didn't argue with Danny anymore, but the disappointment was written indelibly upon his face.

Danny ate with Kay that noon and talked with her about working at the camp.

"The way you can ride," he said, "I'm sure that you could get a job here all summer long. That might help a lot toward going to school next fall."

"Mr. Harmon has already suggested that," she said without enthusiasm. "But you know how little I'd be able to make as a counselor. No, Danny. There just isn't any way out for me."

Marilyn, who was sitting at the same table, straightened suddenly. "I just thought of something, Kay," she exclaimed, her face brightening. "Perhaps Daddy would take on the rest of your support!"

"Oh, I couldn't take it from him," Kay said. "Anyway, I've about given up the idea of going to Bible school."

"Oh, don't, Kay," Marilyn cried. "Daddy's been helping a lot with the missionary program at the church. I'm going to talk to him."

Marilyn went to find her dad as soon as they had finished eating. However, he had gone fishing with one of the men and she didn't get to see him until just before the meeting that night.

"I'd certainly like to be able to help her," he said when Marilyn talked with him. "But I'm already committed as far as our tithe is concerned. I wrote a letter just last week, to one of the large independent mission boards in Africa, telling them that I would take on half of the support of one of their missionaries. I can't go back on that."

Marilyn was crestfallen.

"But Kay is so desperate for help. She isn't going to be able to go to school unless somebody helps her. I'd be willing to go to work here at the camp and send you the money I'd make to go toward her support."

Mr. Forester put his arm about his daughter's shoulders. "Does it mean that much to you?"

She nodded.

"I'll talk to your mother about it tonight and see if we can work out something."

"Do you have to talk to her? You know how she feels about Kay."

Mr. Forester nodded. "Mom and I are partners. I don't like the idea of doing things behind her back, even though the things I plan to do are Christian."

"I suppose you're right," she said, doubtfully.

All during the meeting that night Marilyn was so excited she could scarcely listen. Her mom had stayed in the cabin with a sick headache, as usual, but her dad had come and was sitting on the front row. As soon as the service was over, he ducked out.

"Did you get to talk to your dad?" Danny asked, coming up to Marilyn.

"He's going to talk with Mom tonight."

"Perhaps we had better go over and pray about it."

Chuck Martin was talking with Kay. Danny, Tim, and Marilyn slipped out the side door of the tabernacle and went to a secluded spot in one corner of the clearing where they knelt and prayed. It was almost an hour later when Tim walked back to the Forester cabin with Marilyn.

"We'll keep on praying," he assured her.

Danny Orlis half expected Harold Bauer to come back to the Broken Arrow Bible Camp and make one more attempt to get Ron to go with him on that fishing trip. Ron expected him too.

"If Uncle Harold comes back again," his brother said hotly, "and asks me to take that fishing trip with him, I'm going. I don't care what you say!"

"I don't want to argue with you. But Dad said he didn't want you to go. I can't let you do something against his orders. Harold Bauer is trying to get you and Roxie from us."

Ron's eyes were snapping. "Maybe I'd like that a lot better. At least I'd be able to do some of the things I want to do!"

Danny was uneasy that day and the next. He scarcely let either of the twins out of his sight for more than half an hour. But there was no sign of Harold Bauer.

"I wouldn't worry about it if I were you," Tim said to Danny that evening as the two got ready to go to bed. "I think Harold Bauer was just running a bluff. He'd never dare to snatch the twins."

Danny shook his head doubtfully.

"When he learned that he couldn't scare you into letting Ron go with him, he beat it. He's probably gone back to Colorado."

"I hope you're right," Danny said.

The following morning, he began to feel a little better about it. Harold Bauer didn't show up at the camp and Ron was acting more like himself again. He took part in the camp sessions and entered the swimming races. He even pestered Kay into letting him enroll in the riding class and started to read his Bible once more. Danny happened by his cabin during the rest period after dinner and saw him lying on his bunk, reading his New Testament.

That evening Ron was one of the first into the tabernacle for the evening message.

The speaker spoke on consecration. It was a hard, slugging message that drove to the very depths of Danny's heart. He cast a quick, sidelong glance at his younger brother, Ron, who was squirming uneasily in his seat. Ron bit his lower lip savagely and clenched his fists until his knuckles whitened. When the service was over and the invitation was given for those who wished to take a forward step in consecration, Danny moved over to his brother's side and put his arm about him.

Warning signals flashed in Ron's eyes.

"How about it?" Danny asked softly. "I'm going down to dedicate my whole life to Christ. Will you go with me?"

The younger boy looked away and did not answer.

"What he said is true. We not only need to be saved, but we also need to turn full control of our lives over to the Lord Jesus. We need to surrender our wills to Him and trust Him to guide us. Wouldn't you like to make a decision like that?"

Ron scowled as he winked back the tears.

"Don't put me on the spot, Danny! I'm not ready yet."

CHAPTER 9

UNCLE HAROLD'S PLANS

Roxie Orlis came over to where Danny was standing. "Danny," she said softly, "what was the matter with Ron, anyway?"

"I'm afraid the message tonight was bothering him. I don't know why it's so hard for us to let the Lord Jesus have complete control of our lives. Everyone who takes a stand like that says that it's the only really happy way to live." He paused an instant. "But I guess we're so stubborn and proud that we don't want to let anyone else have control of our lives."

He planned to walk home with Kay that evening but thought he had better go and find Ron instead.

"I think if I can get a chance to talk with him while he's still feeling the effect of this message, Kay," he explained, "I might be able to help him. He was certainly under conviction tonight."

"I'll be praying for him," she said, smiling.

She was still standing there when Chuck Martin came up.

"What happened to the boyfriend? Don't tell me he stood you up tonight."

"He had something much more important to do," she answered.

"I can't think of anything more important than being with you," he said.

"Did they teach you that in college?"

"Really, I am glad that Orlis had to run away. I've been wanting to talk with you alone."

Together they walked out of the tabernacle and across the little path that led to the cabin where Kay was staying.

"What did you think of the message this evening?" she asked presently.

"It makes nice sermon material. But I'm going to keep control of my life. That's one thing sure."

"I can't agree with that, Chuck. The only way a Christian can truly be happy is to turn his life completely over to Christ and let Him do what He wishes with it."

Chuck faced her. "Next, you'll be telling me that you're completely happy. You've consecrated your life and look what happened. You're not even going to be able to go on to school. Is that your idea of the way the Lord takes care of those who turn their lives over to Him? No, sir, I don't want any of it."

Kay tried to find words to explain how she felt now that she had completely settled the matter with the Lord;

to tell him that this was just a time of testing. But somehow, in the face of his bitter anger, her tongue was still.

* * *

The Foresters left for Cedarton early the next morning. Danny and Kay went down to see them off.

"I thought you'd be going back with us, Kay," Mr. Forester said as they stood together on the dock.

"I've decided to stay and work," she said. "I'm going to have to save all the money I can if I'm going to Bible school this fall."

He would have said more to her, but Mrs. Forester called just then, and he turned away.

Danny had a great deal of work to do that morning and almost forgot about Ron and Roxie until afternoon. There was a change of campers that day, and there were no meetings until after dinner that night.

* * *

The packet boat came in about mid-morning and the helper slipped a note to Ron. He sauntered off behind one of the buildings where he stopped and read it. His eyes brightened noticeably and a big smile lighted his face as he read the few short lines. Then, stuffing it into his pocket, he hurried to find Roxie.

"Let's get one of the boats," he whispered, "and slip away for a few minutes."

"But why? What are we going to do?"

"I just got a note from Uncle Harold," he told her secretively. "He wants us to meet him on the other side of the island to talk to him about that big fishing trip we're going to take."

"But Ron," she protested, "we aren't supposed to go anywhere with Uncle Harold."

"Who cares?" he asked. "Uncle Harold said for us to meet him over there at noon. If we don't hurry, he'll think that we're not coming and leave."

"Well," Roxie said reluctantly. "I – I suppose it would be all right."

"Of course, it will be all right." He took her by the hand and guided her down the path. "We've got to hurry or we'll miss him."

It was almost two hours later before Danny, looking around the dining hall, realized that Ron and Roxie weren't there. He got up and went over to the camp director.

"Have you seen the twins?" he asked.

"As a matter of fact, I haven't."

While Danny was still standing there, Cliff Baldwin, one of the counselors, came bursting in.

"Mr. Harmon!" he cried. "One of the boats and a motor are gone!"

For a brief instant, Danny stared at Mr. Harmon and the counselor.

"Are you sure?" he asked weakly.

"I put the motor on the boat this morning so I

could go fishing when I got my work done," Cliff said. "I went to get it just now and the boat and motor are gone!"

"I hardly think that Ron and Roxie would take a boat and run off that way," Danny said thoughtfully, "especially when I told them not to leave."

"I'll go look in the girls' cabins," Mr. Harmon announced. "You two guys check the boys'."

But there was no sign of the twins. Danny and Cliff looked through the dorm, and in two or three of the boys' cabins, but nobody had seen Ron Orlis.

His clothes were just where he had left them, and his Bible was lying on his bunk.

Danny and Cliff went through the tabernacle and the dining hall, and up to the top of the hill where the kids often went to look out over the lake. Icy fingers of fear ran up and down Danny's spine and squeezed his heart until it seemed he couldn't breathe or move. The mail boat had come in that morning. Had Harold been on it to entice the kids away?

"We can't run over this whole island," he said as he and Cliff paused to catch their breath. "Maybe we'd better go back and see if Mr. Harmon has learned anything."

The camp director met them just outside the tabernacle.

"There isn't a sign of them anywhere," he said. "We're going to have to get out a searching party."

"But where do you suppose they could have gone?" Cliff asked.

"We're fortunate that they know something about the lake and the woods," Mr. Harmon observed. "At least they know how to take care of themselves." He turned to Danny. "You don't suppose they got homesick and went back to your place, do you?"

Danny shook his head. "I hardly think so. Of course—," he didn't finish what he had intended to say.

Mr. Harmon called the counselors together and told them what had happened.

"We don't want to get any of our guests excited," he explained. "So, let's go about this search as quietly as possible."

"I think we should get the boats out," somebody suggested, "and look around among the islands. They might have decided to go fishing today. They knew that there wouldn't be much doing in camp."

"And we don't want to forget that they might be on the island, too," Mr. Harmon put in. "They may not have been the ones who took the boat."

"I could pick out two or three good riders," Kay volunteered, "and could comb the island in less time than it could be done on foot."

* * *

At the same time Ron Orlis paddled the white rowboat out into the bay, beyond the little finger of land that screened the camp from the rest of the Lake of the Woods.

"Are you sure we should leave, Ron?" his sister asked uncertainly. "Danny's going to be awfully mad."

"Who cares what Danny thinks? We'll meet Uncle Harold and be back again before anybody ever knows we're gone."

He started the motor and headed around the next little island that lay just behind the one on which the camp was located.

"Let's see now," he said. "Uncle Harold said for us to come around this way and he'd meet us over here."

"I still wish we'd stayed at camp," Roxie protested.

"Oh, don't be so scared," Ron told her, scornfully. "I've got to find out when Uncle Harold and I can make that fishing trip."

Harold Bauer was waiting for them around the island in a sheltered little cove. He was sitting in a powerful launch with an Indian at the wheel. As soon as the kids came into view he waved cheerfully to them.

"Hi, there," he called, "it's so good to see you."

Ron shut off the motor and glided up to the launch. "As soon as I got your letter, I found Roxie and we sneaked over here."

"I knew I could count on you."

"When are we going to make that trip up north?"

"That's what I wanted to talk to you about," Harold Bauer told him. "I thought we'd make it right away."

"But we can't! Danny told us not to!"

Even Ron hesitated a moment. "But Uncle Harold," he said, "I didn't even bring my fishing tackle along, or extra clothes or anything. I – I don't see how we could go now. Maybe tomorrow."

"Don't you worry about those things," Harold Bauer said. "We're going to get you a whole new outfit of clothes up in Kenora. And I'll buy both of you new fishing outfits too."

"Our parents won't like it," Roxie repeated doubtfully.

"It's the only time I could take you." Harold shrugged his shoulders as though he didn't care one way or the other. "I went over and tried to talk to Danny about it, but he acted as though he didn't want you to have any fun at all. He said he was going to see to it that you didn't get to go. I don't think it's your parents. I think it's Danny. He's jealous because we didn't ask him."

Ron bristled. "It sounds just like him," he retorted. He was still thinking about the night before when Danny had come up to talk with him about consecrating his life. "Always wanting to spoil things for a guy."

"Now, Ron," Roxie said loyally. "You know that isn't true."

"Well," their uncle cut in shortly, "if you're going with me, you'd better be getting in the launch."

"You can go ahead if you want to, Ron," Roxie said, drawing away. "I'm not going."

"Don't be such a spoil-sport. We'll be back in two or three days, and we'll catch some of the biggest fish you ever saw."

"Not unless we talk to Danny first."

Harold Bauer reached out and grabbed her by the arm.

"You'd better come along if you know what's good for you," he gritted. Roxie whimpered a little, but she did as she was told.

"That's better," Harold Bauer said, smiling. "You'll never regret taking this trip with me. We'll just pull the boat up on shore where the camp can find it in a few days and we'll be on our way."

They rode several miles in the launch before either of the twins said anything. Finally, Ron asked, "Where are we going, Uncle Harold?"

"Over here to meet a plane," Harold Bauer said.

"And – and then where are we going?" Roxie asked him.

The smile left his face. "I told you once, Roxie. What's the matter? Don't you trust me?"

She said nothing. Instead, she huddled into the corner of the seat and stared down at the floor until finally the boat pulled up alongside the little seaplane that had been landed near one of the islands.

"You're late," the pilot grunted, looking at his watch. "This is going to cost you."

"Don't worry," Harold Bauer retorted, hoisting Roxie into the plane. "You're going to be paid well enough."

"This is risky business," the pilot continued. "I don't like this fooling around where I'm liable to be caught. If you hadn't come in five minutes, I'd have flown off and left you."

"We're here now," Harold Bauer told him.

The pilot, who had been letting the engine idle, revved it up and started to move out toward open water.

"Where are we going?" Roxie asked again, her voice trembling.

Harold Bauer turned to face her. "You'd just as well know it," he snapped. "You're going to Winnipeg with me. You'll never see the Orlises again!"

CHAPTER 10

FLIGHT TO WINNIPEG

The searchers were looking frantically for Ron and Roxie Orlis. Kay and her companions combed the island from one end to the other on horseback. The men in boats covered the area surrounding the island. It was Danny who found the boat and motor, and the old Indian who had taken Harold Bauer and the twins to the plane.

After leaving Mr. Bauer the Indian went back to the place where the camp boat had been left and was taking the motor off it when Danny and Cliff roared around the end of the island in the launch and saw him.

"I was going to take this over to your camp," the guy lied. "Somebody might steal it if it's left out here like this."

"Where are the kids who were in this boat?" Danny demanded.

The old Indian shrugged. "Did you see the airplane a few minutes ago?" he asked.

Danny nodded. He had seen the plane take off less than ten minutes before, nosing up over the trees and heading toward the Northwest.

"They were in it."

"Who was with them? Where were they going?"

The Indian shrugged his shoulders. "Man come to see me. He asked me to bring him here. We meet boat with kids, and all of them go in plane. That all I know!"

"Just as I thought!" Danny cried. "That must have been Harold Bauer! He's got the twins!"

* * *

Ron and Roxie sat silently in the plane as they nosed down to the Winnipeg airport.

"Now, listen," Harold Bauer told them before they got out of the small craft. "You are my niece and nephew. I've got a legal right to have you. It doesn't make any difference if you get in touch with the local police, or anyone else. But I don't want a scene. If you want to get in trouble – either one of you – just make a fuss."

"We won't do anything like that," Ron protested, his voice quavering.

"See that you don't. You're going to stay with me. If you do as I ask you to, we'll get along fine. If you don't there'll be trouble."

On the way to the hotel, their uncle was his usual laughing self again. He joked with the taxi driver and the bell boy who took them up to their room. He even gave Roxie an affectionate little pat on the head as she walked past him.

"I don't want you kids to pay any attention to what I said at the airport a few minutes ago," he told them. "I was so excited and nervous at getting you kids with me again that I guess I hardly knew what to do." He walked over to the dresser and picked up a newspaper. "I'll look in here and see what shows are on tonight," he said presently. "Maybe we can find a good one."

Roxie looked up at Ron.

"We don't care to go to a show, Uncle Harold," Ron told him. "We feel it's better for Christians not to."

Harold Bauer whirled. "Now, don't go to giving me that Christian stuff," he snapped. "You're going to have to get that out of your heads. You're going to be living with me. You'll never see the Orlises again, and we're not going to have trouble with that crazy religion of theirs!" He threw the paper down. "Now, do you want to go to the show or don't you?"

Trembling, Roxie shook her head. Ron did the same.

"All right!" Harold Bauer shouted. "But you're going to have to forget that religion stuff!" He strode out of the room and they heard the key click in the lock.

Ron and Roxie sat there a few moments, staring at one another.

"Ron," his twin said weakly, "what are we going to do?"

"I don't know," he managed to say. "I don't know what we're going to do." He was silent for a long while.

She walked nervously over to the window and back again, but he hadn't moved. He was still sitting there, staring miserably at the floor.

"None of this would have happened," she told him tearfully, "if you hadn't made me go. We should have listened to Danny. I told you we should have stayed at the camp."

"It's my fault, Roxie," Ron said, chewing his lower lip. "If I hadn't been so stubborn and selfish I'd have known Danny was only doing what was best for us when he told me not to go on that fishing trip. But I had to do things my own way. And look what's happened!"

She walked over to the window and looked out on the busy street eight stories below. "What do you suppose Uncle Harold is going to do with us?" Her voice was weak.

"He plans to keep us, that's what!"

She turned back to him. "What can we do, Ron?" she asked plaintively.

There was a long silence. Then, without speaking, Ron dropped to his knees beside the bed.

"O heavenly Father," he began to pray. Roxie came over and knelt beside him. "You know all about Uncle Harold. You know what he is planning to do with us, and why he wanted to take us away from Mom and Dad Orlis. O God, just be with us and help us to get away from him. Help us to get back home to Angle Inlet."

Ron stopped suddenly. For a full minute, they knelt there, breathing heavily. Roxie was too choked to pray aloud. Finally, Ron began again. "O Lord Jesus," he said, his voice hushed and broken, "please forgive me for having to have my own way. Please forgive me for disobeying Dad and Danny, and for getting Roxie into this trouble. She didn't want to go; I made her do it. Forgive me for not wanting to give You control of my life. I see now how messed up I'd get things if I ran things myself. But I want You to take control now!"

Roxie began to pray after Ron, and for a couple of minutes after she had finished, they did not move. Then they got to their feet and for a moment or two, they clung to each other in a tight embrace.

"I feel a little better, Ron," she said to him, her voice hushed.

"I feel a lot better, Roxie. I don't know why I've been so stubborn and so determined to want to run my own life. But I see now what comes of it. I don't know what God will have for me, but I'm going to let Him have control of my life from now on. It's the *only* way to live!"

Roxie went to the telephone and fingered the receiver. "If we just knew somebody here in Winnipeg," she said, "we could phone them and tell them what happened. We could get someone to help us get away from Uncle Harold."

"But we don't know anybody here, Roxie," Ron said. "That's just the trouble."

She went over to the wall radio above one of the beds and switched it on.

"And this is the Wilderness Pastor from Winnipeg," she heard a familiar voice say.

Roxie stiffened suddenly. "Ron!" she exclaimed. "Did you hear that?"

Ron nodded, realizing suddenly what she was talking about. "That's right!" he cried eagerly.

"Dad was telling us about meeting him," he went on. "What was his name, Roxie?"

"I don't remember," she said.

"It was Clarence something or other," Ron went on thoughtfully, muttering more to himself than his sister. "But that won't matter. Let's just call the Wilderness Pastor."

Ron picked up the telephone book and opened it hurriedly, running his finger down the list of names. "Here it is," he said.

Roxie handed him the phone. "Call him, Ron," she said, almost whispering. "I know he'll help us!"

Ron lifted the receiver. "This is room 802," he said, remembering the way he had heard Harold Bauer make a phone call an hour or so before. "Please give me an outside line."

"I'm sorry," the crisp voice from the other end

replied. "But your uncle gave strict orders that you are not to make any phone calls while he is gone."

"But – but – Ron protested lamely.

"I'm sorry," the girl at the switchboard said. With that there was a dull click, and the phone went dead.

"What happened?" Roxie asked quickly.

His face was ashen and his fingers trembled as he set the phone back on its cradle.

"She won't let us call anyone," he whispered, as though the life had suddenly gone out of him. "Uncle Harold left orders that we were not to make any phone calls while he is gone."

CHAPTER 11

DISCOVERED

Harold Bauer had breakfast sent up to the hotel room the following morning and stood over the twins while they ate. He seemed excited and irritable about something. Two or three times he went to the telephone, calling down to the desk to see if there had been any messages for him.

"I told that lawyer to get in touch with me," he muttered to himself as he hung up the phone for the third time. "The trial is coming off the last of the week. I've got to know how things are going."

He turned back to the twins.

"I've got to leave for a while," he said. "When the bell boy comes for the dishes, he has instructions to lock this door after him and see that it's kept locked. You might be interested too to know that there is a house detective stationed on this floor right now to watch you two. You don't have a chance of getting away."

"You don't need to worry about us," Ron answered.

"I know this isn't too good, living in a hotel room this way," Harold Bauer said, changing his manner suddenly. "But it won't be long until we'll be able to move back to Iron Mountain with your Aunt Margaret. Right now, I've got to make sure that the Orlises don't try to get you away from me."

"Do you suppose we could sneak out when the bell boy comes to take these dishes back?" Roxie asked as soon as their uncle was gone.

Ron shook his head.

"I saw that big guy standing at the end of the corridor," he said. "I've got a hunch that Uncle Harold talked with the manager of the hotel. He must have made him think that Danny or someone was trying to kidnap us. We wouldn't stand a chance."

"If we could just get word to somebody."

There was a knock on the door.

"I've got it, Ron," she whispered.

While he went to the door, she sat down at the desk and began to write furiously.

"Would you mail a couple of letters for me, please?" she asked the bell boy.

"Do you have them ready?"

"I will in a minute."

By the time he had finished getting the dishes together, she had scrawled off a note to the Orlises at Angle Inlet, and another to Wilderness Pastor in Winnipeg.

When he was gone Ron looked up at his sister, grinning broadly. "Boy," he said with admiration, "I'd never have thought of that. Now when those letters get to where they're going everything will be all right."

Half an hour or so later Harold Bauer came back to the room.

"Well, kids," he said, "you'd better get your things together. We're going to move."

"Move?" Roxie asked in dismay. "Where to?"

"You'll see soon enough."

And then, smiling crookedly, he threw two letters on the desk in front of her. "By the way, the bell boy gave these to me a minute ago. You didn't think it would be that easy to get word to the Orlises, did you?"

Ron's and Roxie's hearts sank within them!

* * *

Carl Orlis came over to the Broken Arrow Bible Camp as soon as Danny got word to him.

"I should have known that Harold Bauer would try something like this," he said.

"I'm sorry, Dad," Danny replied. "I tried to keep them from him."

Carl put an arm around his son's shoulder. "Don't feel so bad about it, Danny. You did the best you could."

"But what can we do?" Danny asked. "We can't let him get away with it."

"I think I'll go to Warroad and see the lawyer again," Mr. Orlis answered. "The other day when I talked with him, he said that everything was going splendidly for us. He has been able to get some affidavits in Iron Mountain as to Harold Bauer's character, and the character of his wife, to say nothing of evidence that Harold had plenty of notice of the hearing in which the twins were awarded to us." He shook his head. "If we had just been able to keep them out of his hands, everything would have been all right."

Danny choked suddenly. "How is Mom taking it?"

"She's holding up real well. She asked me to tell you that she didn't blame you, and to ask you to keep praying."

Danny Orlis went through the motions of doing his work, but somehow, he couldn't keep his mind on it, or on the messages he heard. Kay came over at noon and ate with him.

"I just wanted you to know, Danny, that I've been praying for you."

"Thanks."

Chuck Martin came up just then.

"Boy, it's tough about your kid brother and sister, Danny. Have you heard anything from them?"

"Not a word," he replied. "Dad figures that Bauer is holding them somewhere up there in Canada."

Mr. Harmon, the camp director, sent word for Danny to come to his office just then. When he left the table, Chuck turned to Kay.

"Well," he said, "what have you decided about next fall?"

"I'm leaving the whole matter in the hands of the Lord, Chuck."

"Now, what do you mean by that?"

"I've been praying about it, and I feel that God would have me go to Bible school. So, I'm saving every penny I can, and I'm going ahead with my plans to attend the Bible institute in Cedarton, trusting in the Lord to provide the money."

He looked at her in amazement. "You don't really mean that, do you? You don't expect to have the money handed to you, just like that!"

"I don't know how the money is coming, but I expect to go to Bible school."

"And if you don't?" he asked her. "If God doesn't provide, what then?"

She toyed with her spoon.

"If He doesn't provide for me to go to Bible school, Chuck," she said softly, "I will know that it wasn't His will that I go there."

He was still staring at her. "You mean it's as simple as that to you?"

"I've had a terrific battle with myself about this thing," she confessed, "but I see now that there's only one way to live a happy Christian life. That is to let Him have full control and trust Him to work out what is best for us."

"You make it sound mighty inviting," Chuck answered wistfully.

That evening the speaker brought another message on consecration, and when the invitation was given Chuck Martin was the first person to stand.

"When I saw how serene and content you are, Kay," he explained to her later, "I saw that I'd been all wrong about wanting to keep control of my life. I'm going to let the Lord Jesus have full control now."

* * *

Harold Bauer took the twins across Winnipeg to a big, rambling three-story boarding house almost on the edge of town. The landlady was tall and bony, with a perpetual scowl on her sharp face.

"You don't need to worry about your niece and nephew, Mr. Bauer," she assured him. "I've taken care of a lot of kids in my time. They won't give me any trouble."

"That will be fine, Mrs. Scroggins," he said. "I don't want them to see anyone, or write any letters, or talk to anyone over the phone. I'm going to be gone for a few days. I want to be sure they both will be here when I get back. I'll need them at the time of the trial."

"You don't need to worry about them," she answered. "They'll be here when you get back."

Harold Bauer ate at the boarding house with the twins and ten or twelve others who roomed there. When he finished, he got to his feet.

"I'll be down to see you in the morning before I leave town," he told Ron and Roxie. "If there's anything you want, I'll get it for you then."

As soon as he was out of sight, Mrs. Scroggins shooed Ron and Roxie up to their rooms. "I don't want to hear a thing out of you," she ordered sternly. "Now stay up there and do as I say."

She put the twins in adjoining rooms with a door between them. As soon as she had gone, Ron threw the bolt on his side of the door and called Roxie to do the same. In a moment they were together again.

"Do you suppose there's any chance of getting out of here?" Roxie whispered, looking anxiously about.

"That's just what I was wondering." He went to the window and glanced out at the darkened street. "We're quite a ways from the ground. I thought maybe if we could –" he stopped quickly.

There, just outside the window, was a little ledge that ran over to the porch roof.

"Roxie," he said excitedly, "do you suppose we could follow along that ledge over to the roof of the porch?"

She examined it, shivering. "I – I don't know," she said uncertainly.

"But if we could make it, we could climb down the rose trellis to the ground. We could get away, Roxie!"

"I – I'll try," she said. "I'm scared to death, but I'll try."

Quickly they knelt together at the windowsill, praying.

"O heavenly Father," Roxie prayed, her voice quivering with fear and excitement. "Be with us now as we climb out onto that ledge. Help us get to the ground safely, and over to the Wilderness Pastor before Uncle Harold catches us. Help us to get back home to Angle Inlet with Mom, Dad, and Danny."

Ron prayed when she had finished and the two of them got to their feet. He raised the window cautiously and loosened the screen.

"Maybe you had better go first, Roxie," he whispered. "Whatever you do be careful."

"Don't worry about me being careful," she said, gasping. But, in spite of the fact that she was so frightened that her heart was beating a fierce tattoo against her ribs, she climbed noiselessly out of the window onto the little ledge. It was pitch black outside, so dark that unless she stopped and stared down, she couldn't even see the ground. Slowly, step by step, she inched her way along, not daring to think about the distance below them, not daring to think what would happen if Harold Bauer chanced to drive up before they got down.

She had crawled some ten or twelve feet when a car went by on the street below. She froze where she was, pressing tightly against the building.

"Take it easy, Roxie," Ron whispered. "I'm right behind you."

Finally, although it seemed as though they had been on the ledge for hours, they reached the rain spout and the porch roof.

"Are you all right?" Ron whispered in her ear.

She nodded.

"Come over here," he said. "I noticed this trellis when we came up."

The trellis was made of heavier lumber than most, and it held Ron's weight easily. An instant or two later they were both on the ground.

"I think we'd better go," Ron said, panting heavily. "Old Mrs. Scroggins is apt to miss us at any minute and come charging out to look for us."

Roxie shivered involuntarily. Together they stole cautiously out to the alley and across the street.

"Where do you suppose we should go?" Roxie asked when they were a block and a half from the house.

"Do you remember the address of the place where Mr. Reimer, the Wilderness Pastor, lived?" Ron asked her.

"Sure," Roxie answered. "I remember it from the letter I wrote him the other day."

"If we can find him, I know he'll help us."

They walked hurriedly up the street until they found a store that was still open. The proprietor directed them to Mr. Reimer's home.

"But aren't you kids too young to be out so late at night?" he asked.

"I guess it is a little late," Ron said, "but we want to get to his place if we can."

"You're going to have to do some walking, but if you follow the directions, you should get there all right."

They went out into the chill night air once more and walked hurriedly, excitedly, along the street.

"Where do you suppose Uncle Harold is?" Roxie asked.

Ron shook his head. "And I don't want to know. Do you suppose Mrs. Scroggins has missed us by now?"

"If she has," Roxie said, "she'll be out looking for us."

Finally, they reached the street and knocked at the house where Clarence Reimer lived.

"It's sure dark!" Roxie muttered under her breath. "Do you suppose he's home?"

Ron did not answer, but his heart quickened its pace. "We'll soon find out."

And then, as they stood together on the porch, a car came slowly by.

"Roxie!" Ron warned, but before they could move, a spotlight on the car was switched on and caught them in its blazing stare.

"I thought I'd find you here!" Harold Bauer exclaimed angrily.

CHAPTER 12

RON'S DISCOVERY AND DECISION

Ron and Roxie Orlis cringed in the blinding glare of the spotlight, not daring to move.

"What shall we do?" Roxie gasped, her voice trembling.

Her twin brother took a step forward uncertainly.

By this time Harold Bauer had leaped from his car and was running toward them.

"I'm sure glad I kept that letter you tried to mail. I knew just where to look for you. You'll be sorry you ever tried to run away from me," he snarled, "when I get through with you!"

"Run, Roxie!" Ron ordered.

"There – there's no place to run!"

At that instant, the porch light was snapped on and the door opened.

"What's going on out here?" a voice in the doorway demanded sternly.

Mr. Reimer's sudden appearance stopped Harold Bauer momentarily.

"I – I – ," he began.

The moment the door opened, Roxie opened the screen door and popped inside.

With a lunge forward, Harold Bauer grasped Ron by the wrist.

"Let go of me!" he cried.

Mr. Reimer ran to the steps and wrenched Harold's hand from Ron's wrist. "Take your hands off him!" he ordered. "I don't know who these youngsters are, but they're on my property, so leave them alone."

"They ran away from me!" Harold Bauer retorted savagely. "I'm responsible for them."

"No, he isn't," Roxie said hurriedly. "We're Ron and Roxie Orlis. Uncle Harold took us away from Mom and Dad Orlis, and he's trying to keep us. But we want to go back home. We don't want to stay with him."

"Wait until I get my hands on you!" Harold Bauer threatened.

"I don't know that you'll get your hands on them at all, Mister," Clarence Reimer told him firmly.

"But they're my brother's kids," Mr. Bauer repeated. "I've been trying to make them behave. They got angry and ran away. That's the whole trouble. What they need is a good tanning."

"Don't let him take us," Roxie pleaded. "If you do, we'll never get to see Mom and Daddy again."

"Don't you worry," Mr. Reimer answered her. "He's not going to take you until we hear the whole story."

At that moment, a neighbor stepped out. "What's all the noise out here?"

Harold Bauer interrupted. "These kids are giving me trouble."

"Do you want me to call the police, Clarence?" the neighbor asked.

Harold Bauer straightened suddenly, muttered under his breath, and strode off the porch.

"Why don't we go into the living room now?" the pastor said, "and we'll hear the whole story right from the beginning. I wish my wife were here. But she's visiting her parents down in Steinbach for a few days, so I'm all alone."

When he heard the whole story, he got to his feet and walked to the telephone. "I think we'd better get in touch with the police. We'll see what they suggest."

"They won't make us go back to him, will they?" Ron asked, his voice tense with concern.

When Mr. Reimer had finished talking with the authorities, he turned back to the twins. "It's just as I thought," he said. "Harold Bauer would have to go to court to prove that he is your legal guardian if you aren't in his custody. And I'm sure he won't try that."

For a long minute, the twins sat there, staring at

one another. Tears welled full in Roxie's eyes, and Ron was strangely choked.

"Isn't it wonderful the way God has worked things out for us?" Roxie asked when she could speak. "Just think! Uncle Harold brought us to the one place in Canada where we could find someone to help us."

Her brother nodded.

"You know, Mr. Reimer," Ron said, "we've been praying and praying about getting away from Uncle Harold. We couldn't figure out any way to do it. He had it fixed at the hotel so we couldn't phone or write letters to anyone. And at the boarding house he had that Mrs. Scroggins watching us. We didn't know what to do."

"Except," Roxie added, "to trust Jesus."

Mr. Reimer smiled.

"That's the way it is so many times," he said. "We get to a place where we can't do anything in our own strength, except turn to Christ. What we really should do, all the time, is turn to Him first."

They sat for several minutes, not saying much.

"I suppose you kids will be wanting to get back to Angle Inlet as quickly as you can, won't you?"

"Oh, yes," the twins chorused. "It seems as though it's months since we saw our parents."

"We shouldn't wait around here any longer," Mr. Reimer said. "Your uncle knows where you are now. And even if the police won't do anything to get you away from here for him, there's no telling what he might do."

"I'd never thought of that," Ron answered.

"We'll start for Warroad right away."

Roxie Orlis' face beamed.

* * *

Back at the Broken Arrow Bible Camp, Kay Milburn had packed her bags and was starting down the path toward the dock to catch the boat to Warroad when Chuck Martin came up.

"Good morning," he sang out pleasantly. "May I carry something for you?"

"This bag is a little heavy," she said, smiling. He took her suitcases, letting her carry her light coat and purse.

"Where are you going to be this fall?" he asked presently. "At Cedarton Bible Institute?"

The smile faded from her face.

"I'd like to be," she told him, "but I'm afraid I'm going to have to go back to Mexico."

"How come?"

"The same thing that bothers most missionary kids," she told him. "No money."

They had halted as they started to talk, and Chuck set the suitcases on the ground.

"It's strange too," she went on; "I was so sure the money would come in."

He eyed her quizzically.

"Now tell me the truth," he said. "Aren't you bitter about it?"

She shook her head.

"At first, I was terribly bitter. I got to the point where I was angry because Mom and Dad had been chosen to serve Christ on the mission field. Then I saw that I had to put my trust in the Lord and let Him work out what is best for my life. Now I'm perfectly content to do whatever He wants me to, whether it's back to Mexico or on to Bible school."

Chuck shook his head. "You make me ashamed of myself for the way I've been all these years. I've been bitter about being a missionary's kid too. Only I think I've been bitter about it all my life. The other night I settled the whole matter with the Lord. I'm going to serve Him from now on."

"That's wonderful," she replied.

"But tell me," he asked, "aren't you going to admit that you feel bad about not getting to go to Cedarton to Bible school?"

"Of course I do," she said frankly. "All my friends are going to be there. And Danny is –" she stopped suddenly, blushing.

Chuck noticed and grinned broadly but said nothing.

"If God stops me from going to Bible school this year, it's because He has something else that He wants me to do – something that is better for me."

"Your wanting to go to Bible school so badly has sort of got me interested. Maybe I'll stop by Cedarton on my way home and see what the place looks like. It must be some school!"

"Oh, it is," she told him. "I know you'd love it. They've got a group of wonderful, Spirit-filled teachers, and the best bunch of kids you ever saw. You'd enjoy every minute of it."

They walked on down to the dock and sat down to wait. They had been there only a minute or so when the camp director came up to them.

"Good morning, Kay," he said. "We've been looking all over for you."

"I've been getting my things together," she said. "I'm leaving on the boat this morning, you know."

"This airmail letter came in," Mr. Harmon told her.

Her hand was trembling as she took the envelope.

"Why, it's from Cedarton," she said, "but I don't recognize the handwriting."

"It's probably from an old boyfriend you've forgotten all about," Chuck grinned. "Or don't you have any boyfriends besides Orlis?"

"Oh, be quiet." The color came up into her cheeks again. "I can't even open the envelope with you standing there grinning at me."

"Don't let me bother you," Chuck said. "I'll be as quiet as a little mouse as I peek over your shoulder."

By this time, she had opened the letter and began to read.

"What's the matter?" Chuck asked seriously.

She could not answer him. But when she looked up, her eyes were luminous with tears.

"What is it?" he asked softly.

"It's from Mr. Forester," she said when she could speak. "He's Marilyn's dad, you know. He wrote to tell me that he and his wife have decided to take on the balance of my support. He's going to see that I get to go to Bible school!"

"Wonderful!"

"But I can't understand Mrs. Forester wanting to do anything like that," Kay said. "I don't understand it."

* * *

It was 6:30 in the morning, and Tex had just landed on Pine Creek.

"Oh, Carl!" Mrs. Orlis cried, her voice quavering. "Danny! The twins are back!"

She gathered them into her arms, and for a couple of minutes, nobody could speak.

"Mr. Reimer brought us in his car last night," Ron said later, when they were all sitting in the dining room around the big table having breakfast. "We left just as soon as he found out that Uncle Harold didn't have any legal hold on us."

"How can we ever thank you?" Mrs. Orlis exclaimed, her eyes filling with tears.

Mr. Reimer smiled at her. "It's thanks enough to see how happy you are," he said.

* * *

Several days later, Danny loosened the stern line on the *Vigilante* as she backed off and the fellow on the boat hauled it in. Then the *Vigilante* rounded the Orlis dock to enter the channel for her trip back to American Point, Oak Island, and Warroad.

Ron came up beside Danny and they waved to the two-man crew of the little packet boat as she plowed around the little wooden buoys and circled the weed bed on her way to the Point.

"Dad told me something I think you'd like to know," the younger boy said, smiling. "He was over at the Bible camp last night. They said that Kay is going to get to go to the Bible institute at Cedarton."

Danny stopped, trying to wipe the smile from his face.

"That's nice."

Ron turned to look at him. "Is that all that you've got to say?"

"What did you expect me to say?"

"I expected more than that out of you," Ron told him, "after the way you've been moping around about Kay having to go back to Mexico. You've been acting like somebody died or something. Now when you find out she's going to Cedarton, all you say is, 'That's nice.' I don't get it!"

Danny looped his arm around Ron's shoulder, and together they walked up toward the house.

"That goes to show you, Ron," he said after a moment or two, "how the Lord takes care of us. Kay worried so much about whether she was even going to get to go on to school. I guess for a while she got to feeling as though God did not care about her. Then she decided to leave the whole thing in His hands. Now the matter is all settled."

Ron was silent.

"Know something, Danny?" he said at last. "I learned a lot on this deal with Uncle Harold this summer."

Danny looked at him quizzically. "What do you mean?"

"I've learned that there's only one way for a guy to live. That is to turn his life completely over to the Lord."

"I'm glad to hear you say that, Ron," Danny said. "Actually, Ron, taking Christ as Savior is just the beginning. We can't possibly live triumphant Christian lives until we turn ourselves completely over to Him."

"This whole mess with Uncle Harold wouldn't have happened if I had been living for Christ the way I should have."

"You'll have a lot of problems in school this year. There are a lot of things going on in high school that will hurt your testimony if you take part in them, so you're really going to have to live close to the Lord, Ron."

Mrs. Orlis came to the door and called them into breakfast.

"Danny," Ron said softly as they got to their feet, "it scares me to think of going to high school down there, away from our parents and everything. I don't think I could do it if I didn't know you would be close by in Bible school. You'll help me and pray for me, won't you?"

"Sure thing," his older brother smiled.

Roxie was busy helping her mom get things packed so they could leave for Cedarton the following morning. Danny and Ron helped Mr. Orlis get in a big load of wood and dry-dock the little cabin cruiser that they wouldn't be using again until spring.

"How about going fishing once more before we leave?" Ron asked when the work was finally done. "I'd like to go over and tie into some of those big walleyes in the bay back of Little McCoy. It's going to be a long time before we'll get to fish out there again."

"You took the words right out of my mouth, fella," Danny said. "Get your rod, and let's go."

Together they strode down to the dock.

THE DANNY ORLIS SERIES

The Danny Orlis series, by Bernard Palmer, delivers a blend of adventure, mystery, and suspense through various settings—from the Canadian wilderness to Guatemalan jungles. Danny Orlis, an adept outdoorsman, skilled athlete, and committed Christian, employs his quick thinking, calm bravery, and biblical solutions to confront everyday problems and hair-raising dangers. Early stories focus on Danny navigating school life, sports, and outdoor challenges, while in later books, Danny and his wife Kay provide wisdom and guidance to youngsters facing lifelike situations and challenges. Having sold over two million copies, this series has made Palmer a renowned author in Christian youth literature. Palmer is also the author of the Felicia Cartright series and various other series for Christian youth.

AVAILABLE FROM WWW.ANEKOPRESS.COM

www.ingramcontent.com/pod-product-compliance
Lightning Source LLC
Chambersburg PA
CBHW070912100726
47907CB00008B/2292